Reproducible emergent readers to make and take home

By Jean Warren

Illustrated by Cora Walker-Carleson and Kelly McMahon

Totline® Publications would like to thank Marie Wheeler of Tacoma, WA, for contributing *A is for Apple, B is for Ball* to this book.

Managing Editor: Kathleen Cubley
Contributing Editors: Gayle Bittinger, Elizabeth McKinnon, Susan M. Sexton
Proofreader: Miriam Bulmer
Graphic Design (Interior): Kathy Kotomaimoce
Layout Artist: Gordon Frazier, Sarah Ness
Graphic Design (Cover): Brenda Mann Harrison
Editorial Assistant: Durby Peterson
Production Manager: Melody Olney

Parts of this book have been previously published by Totline® Publications as *Totline "Take-Home" Books—Alphabet & Number Rhymes.*

ISBN: 1-57029-277-9

Library of Congress Catalog Card Number 98-61314

Printed in the United States of America
Published by Totline® Publications

Business Office: 23740 Hawthorne Blvd.
Torrance, CA 90505

Introduction

Young children who are just becoming interested in books and reading are usually long on enthusiasm and short on ability. Totline® Reproducible Rhyme Books are designed to capture that enthusiasm.

Each of the beginning emergent readers in *Alphabet Rhymes* reinforces beginning alphabet concepts and is written in repetitive rhyme. The unique feature of these rhymes is that young children are able to "read" them, using the pictures as their guides. This happens because each rhyme is simply written and illustrated with beginning readers in mind. After reading a book with an adult a few times, your children will be able to read it by themselves.

All of the books in this series are reproducible, so each child can have his or her own copy. Watch your students glow with pride and a feeling of accomplishment as they take home their own books to "read" to their families.

Contents

The page numbers listed above are on the inside margins of each page.

How to Use Totline® Reproducible Rhyme Books

1. Tear out the pages for the book of your choice.
2. For double-sided copies, copy the odd-numbered pages on the front of the paper and the appropriate even-numbered pages on the back, and then cut the pages in half. For single-sided copies, simply copy the pages and cut them in half.
3. Give each child two 5½-by-8-inch pieces of construction paper to use for book covers. Let the children decorate their books covers as desired or use one of the suggestions listed below.
4. If desired, place the book pages on a table and let the children help collate them into books. (Younger children may need help with this process.)
5. Help the children bind their books using a stapler or a hole punch and paper fasteners.

Cover Decorating Ideas

1. Let the children use rubber stamps or stickers that correspond to the rhyme's subject to decorate the covers of the books.

2. Cut sponges into appropriate shapes. Let the children use the sponges like stamps to print designs on their book covers.

3. Make paint pads by folding paper towels, placing them in shallow containers, and pouring small amounts of tempera paint on them. Give the children cookie cutters in the appropriate shapes. Have them dip their cookie cutters into the paint and then press them on the covers of their books.

5. Let the children cut out and glue appropriate magazine pictures on their book covers.

6. Have the children write their names on the backs of their books.

Extended Learning Ideas

1. Enlarge the pages of a book on a photocopier to make a big book. Let the children color the illustrations on the pages.

2. Incorporate the books into a larger seasonal theme unit.

3. Let your children find and color the main object in a story. Then, have them color the rest of the pictures.

4. Add lines for writing to the bottom of each of the pages of a story (see example below). On the writing lines, use dotted lines to print the name of the object the theme object is "on." For example, print the word "flowers" if the story says "Butterflies on the flowers." Photocopy a classroom set of the story. Let your children trace over the printed word on each page.

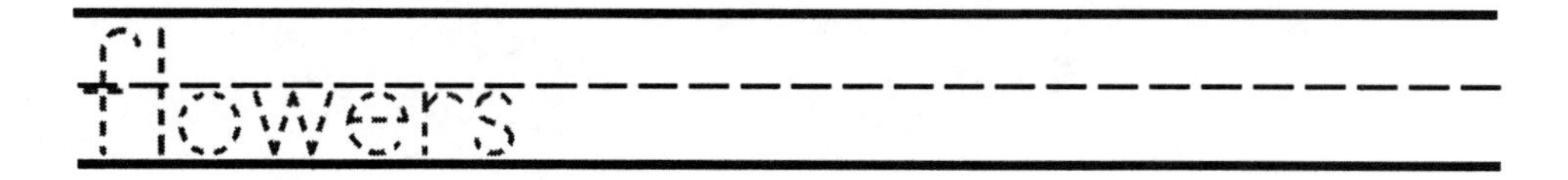

Aa

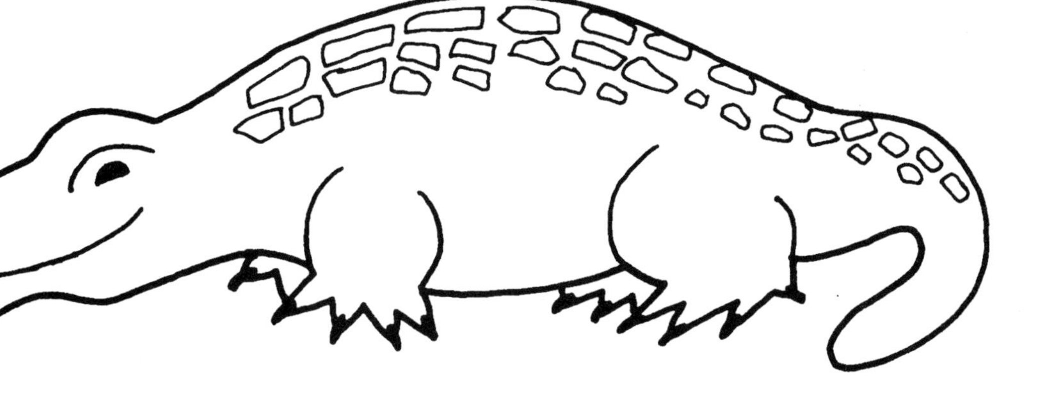

A is for alligator.

Aa

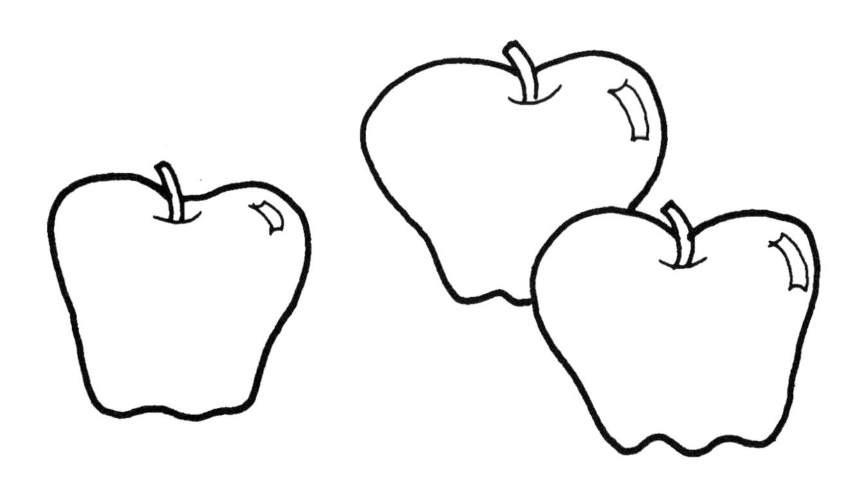

A is for apples

Aa

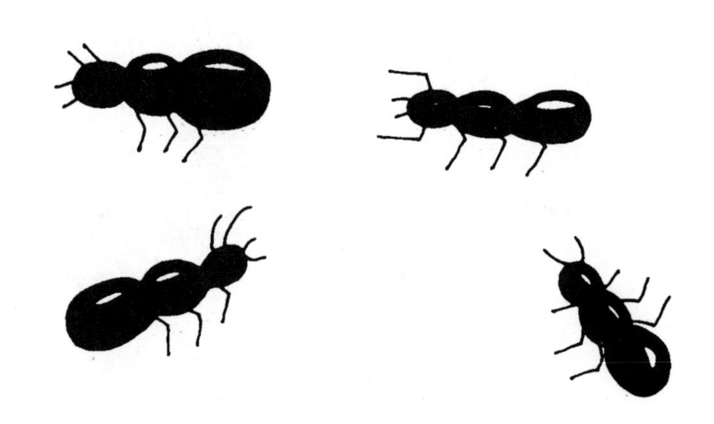

A is for ants.

Aa

on my pants.

Bb

B is for bear.

Bb

B is for buttons

Bb

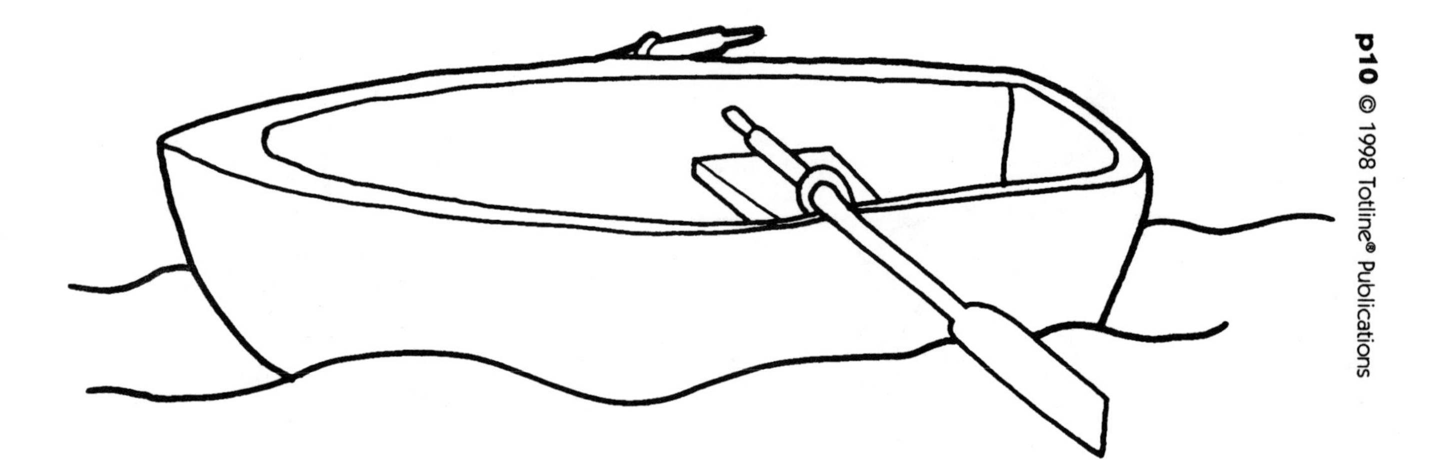

p10 © 1998 Totline® Publications

B is for boat.

Bb

p10 © 1998 Totline® Publications

on my coat.

C is for cow.

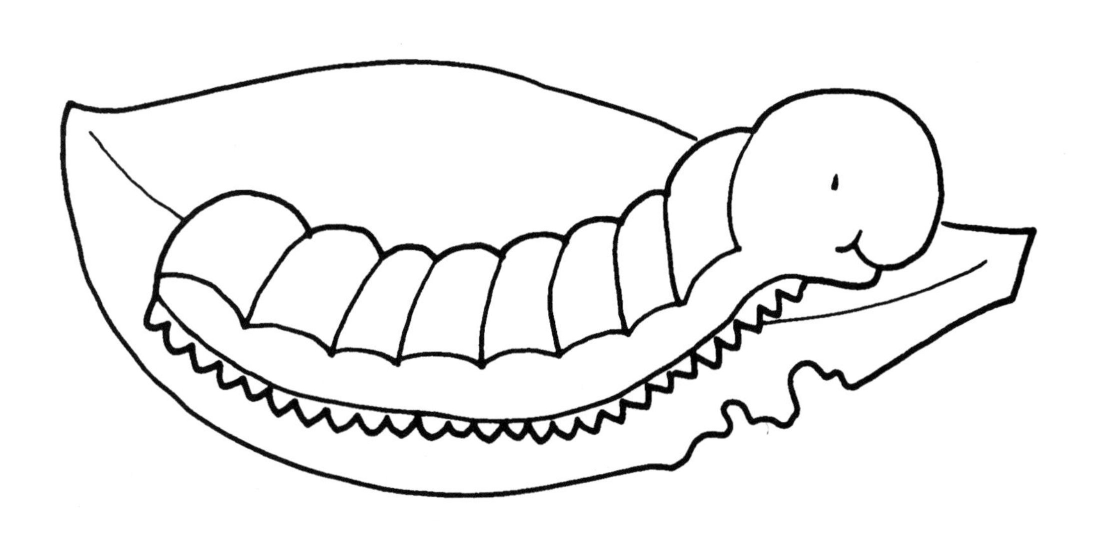

C is for caterpillar

Cc

C is for cat.

Cc

on my hat.

Dd

D is for dinosaur.

Dd

D is for doll

Dd

D is for dog.

p14 © 1998 Totline® Publications

Dd

on my log.

p14 © 1998 Totline® Publications

Ee

E is for envelope.

Ee

E is for elephant

Ee

E is for eggs.

p16 © 1998 Totline® Publications

Ee

on my legs.

p16 © 1998 Totline® Publications

Ff

F is for fire engine.

F is for fox

Ff

F is for fish.

p18 © 1998 Totline® Publications

Ff

in my dish.

p18 © 1998 Totline® Publications

Gg

G is for girl.

Gg

G is for gorilla

Gg

G is for goat.

Gg

in my boat.

Hh

H is for horse.

Hh

H is for hippopotamus

Hh

H is for hair.

on my chair.

Ii

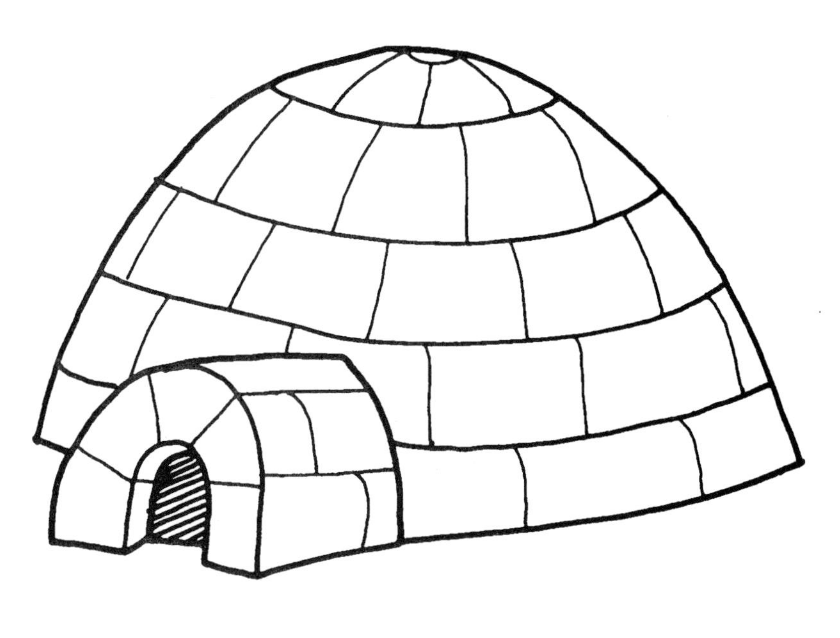

I is for igloo.

I is for iguana

Ii

I is for ink.

p24 © 1998 Totline® Publications

Ii

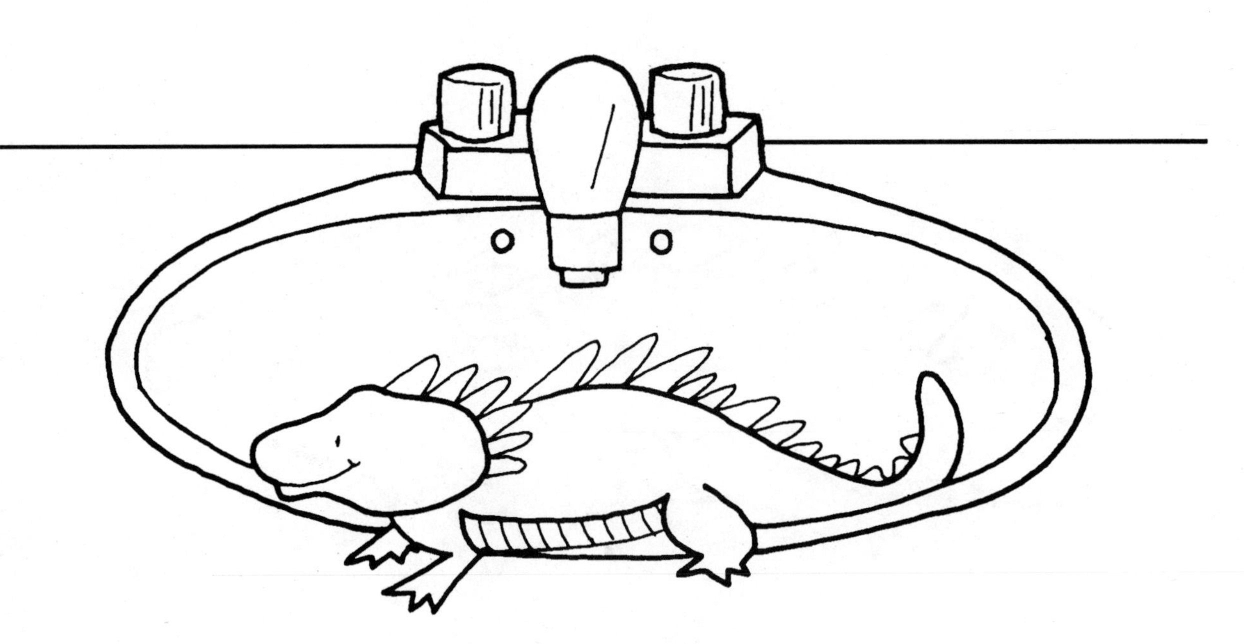

in my sink.

p24 © 1998 Totline® Publications

Jj

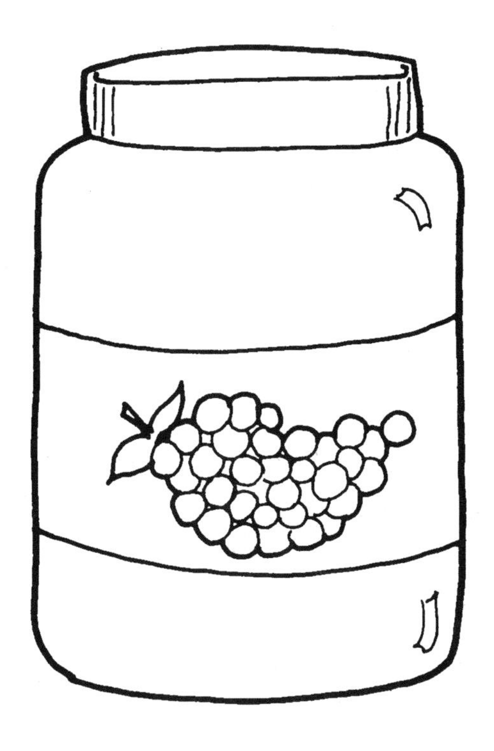

J is for jelly.

Jj

J is for jacket

Jj

J is for jeep.

p26 © 1998 Totline® Publications

Jj

on my sheep.

p26 © 1998 Totline® Publications

Kk

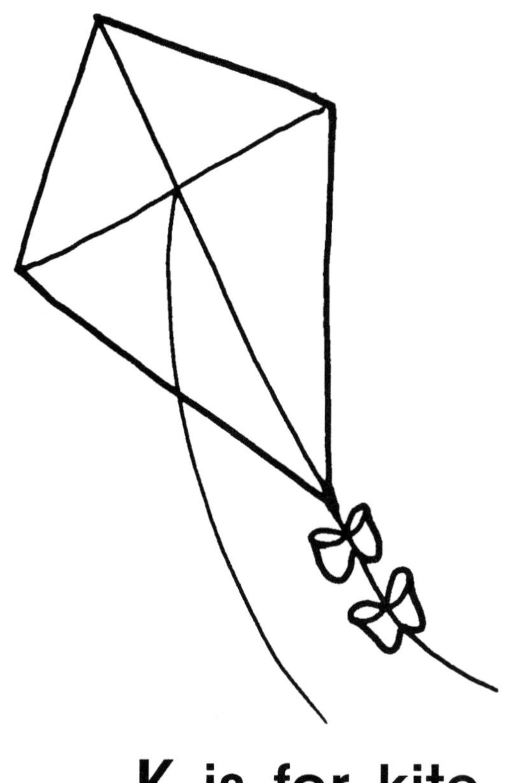

K is for kite.

41

K is for key

43

Kk

K is for king.

Kk

on my string.

Ll

L is for lion.

Ll

L is for leaves

Ll

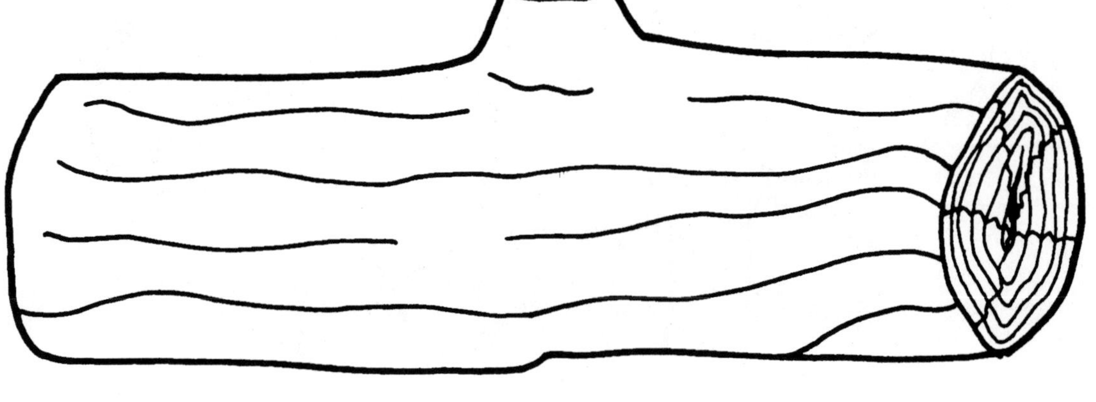

46

L is for log.

p30 © 1998 Totline® Publications

Ll

48

on my frog.

p30 © 1998 Totline® Publications

Mm

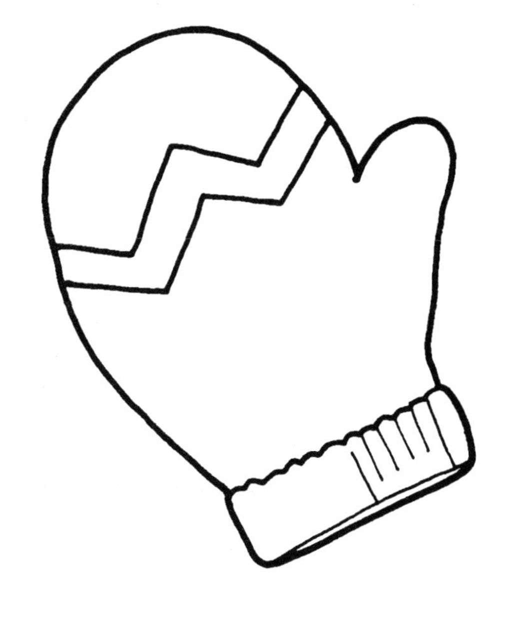

M is for mittens.

49

Mm

M is for monkeys

51

Mm

M is for mouse.

p32 © 1998 Totline® Publications

Mm

on my house.

p32 © 1998 Totline® Publications

Nn

N is for newspaper.

Nn

N is for numbers

Nn

N is for nest.

Nn

on my vest.

p34 © 1998 Totline® Publications

54

p34 © 1998 Totline® Publications

56

O is for octopus.

57

O is for ostrich

59

Oo

58 O is for ox.

p36 © 1998 Totline® Publications

Oo

60 in my box.

p36 © 1998 Totline® Publications

Pp

P is for pizza.

Pp

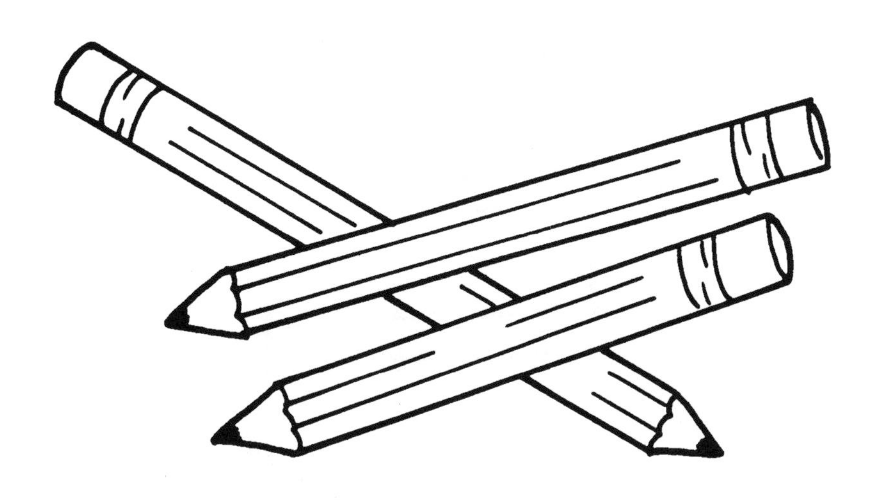

P is for pencils

Pp

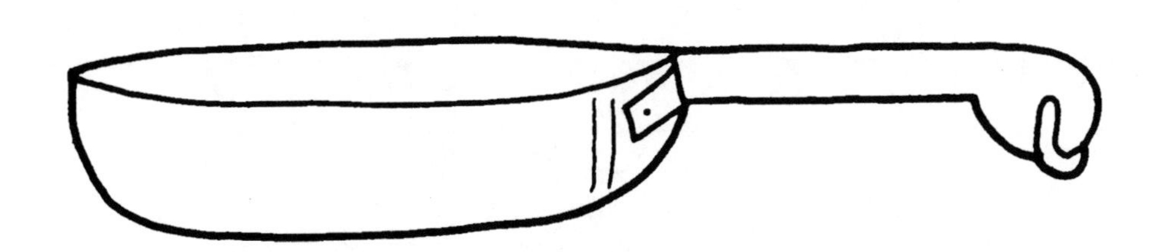

P is for pan.

Pp

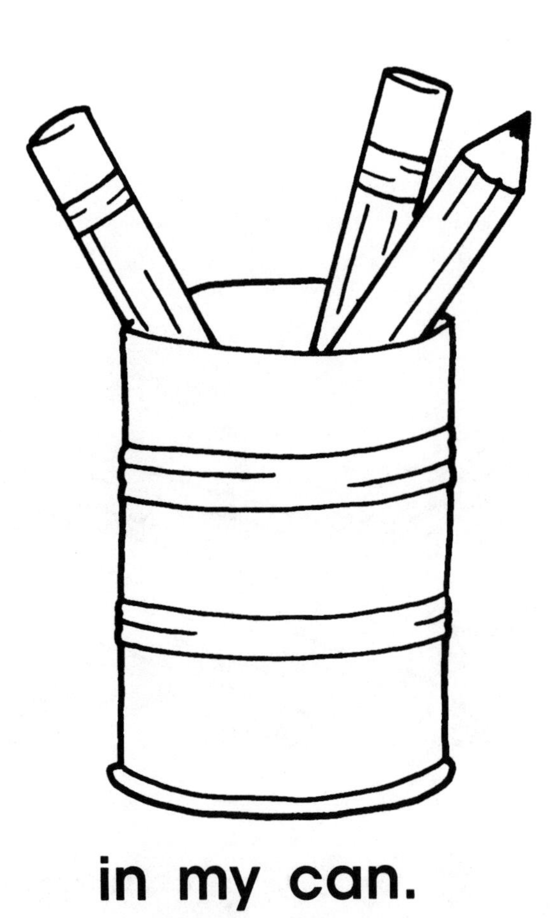

in my can.

Q is for queen.

p39 © 1998 Totline® Publications

Q is for quarters

66

Q is for quail.

Qq

68

in my pail.

Rr

R is for rose.

R is for rabbit

Rr

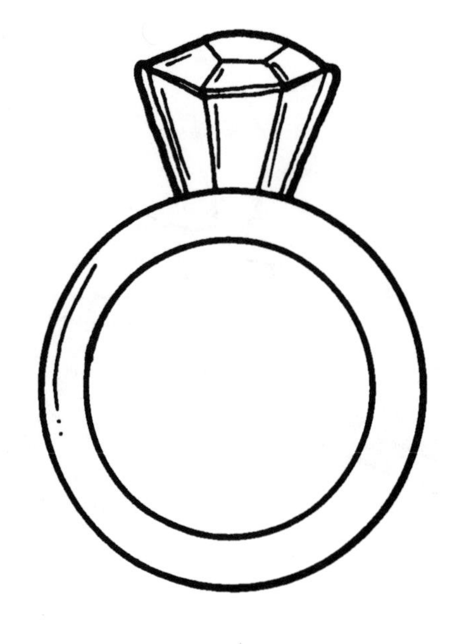

R is for ring.

p42 © 1998 Totline® Publications

Rr

on my swing.

p42 © 1998 Totline® Publications

Ss

S is for sun.

Ss

S is for snails

Ss

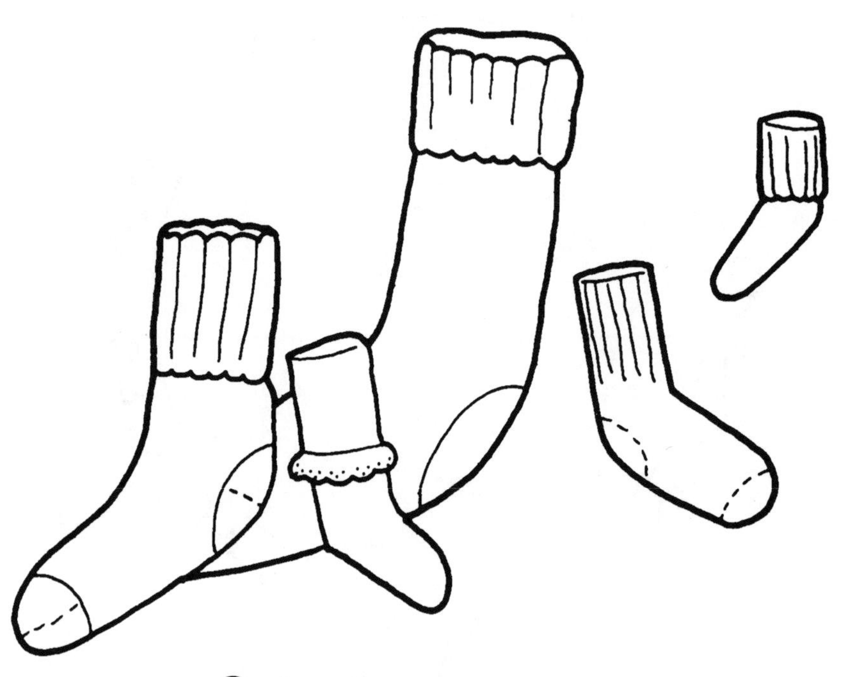

S is for socks.

Ss

on my blocks.

Tt

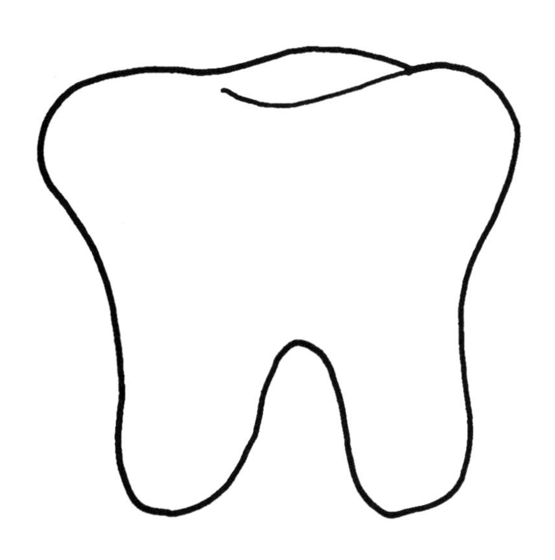

T is for tooth.

Tt

T is for tie

Tt

78 T is for truck.

Tt

80 on my duck.

p46 © 1998 Totline® Publications

Uu

U is for underwear.

Uu

U is for umbrella

82

U is for up.

p48 © 1998 Totline® Publications

Uu

84

in my cup.

p48 © 1998 Totline® Publications

V is for violin.

85

Vv

V is for violets

87

Vv

V is for van.

Vv

in my pan.

Ww

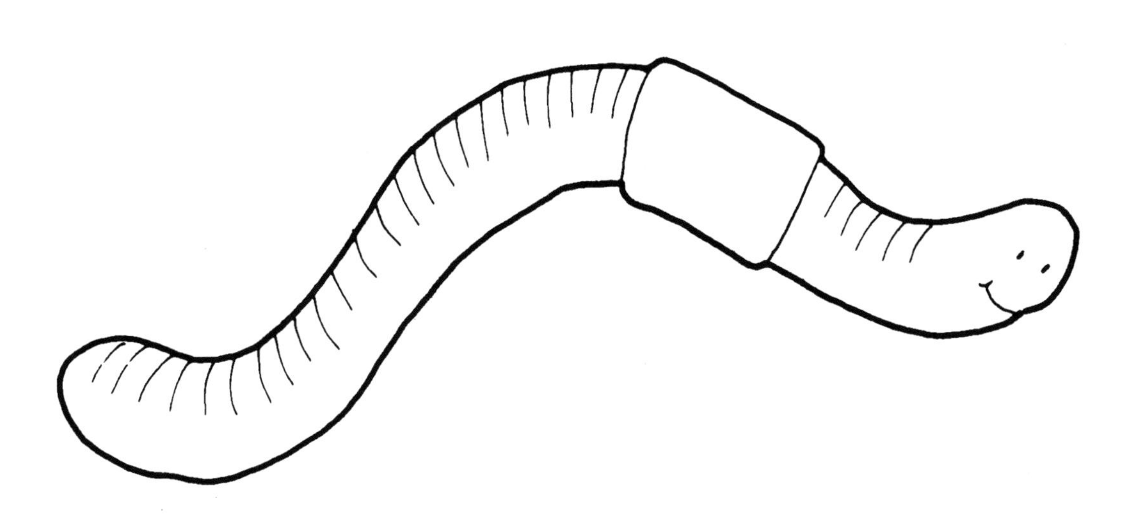

W is for worm.

Ww

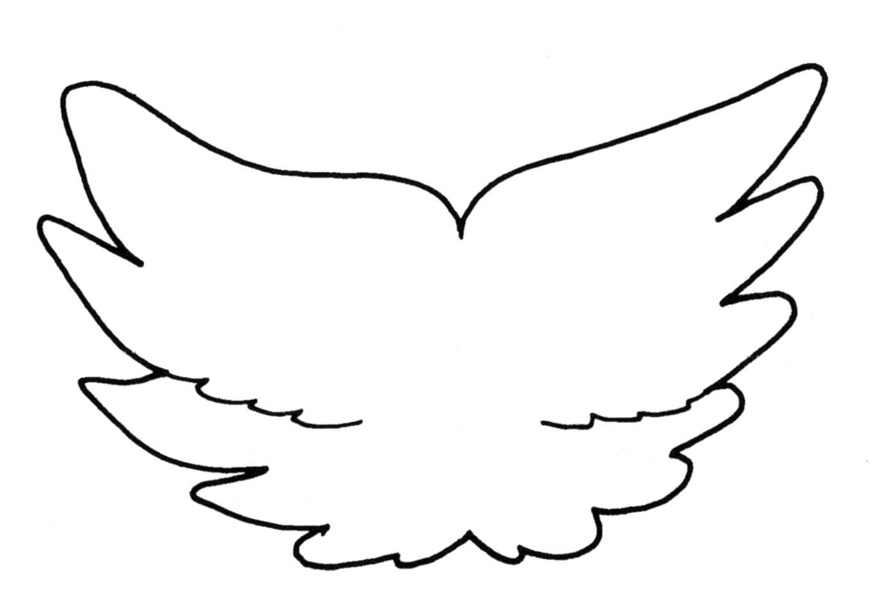

W is for wings

Ww

W is for wagon.

p52 © 1998 Totline® Publications

Ww

on my dragon.

p52 © 1998 Totline® Publications

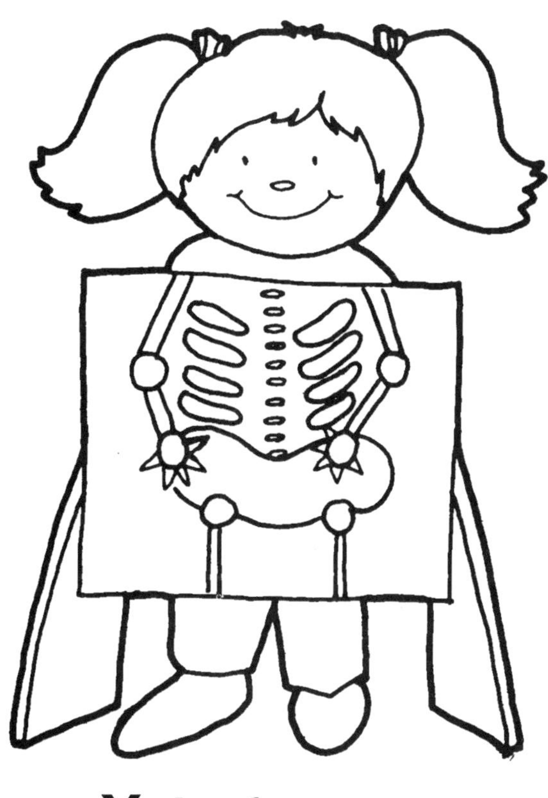

X is for x-ray.

X is for kisses

X marks the spot.

I have a lot.

Yy

Y is for yo-yo.

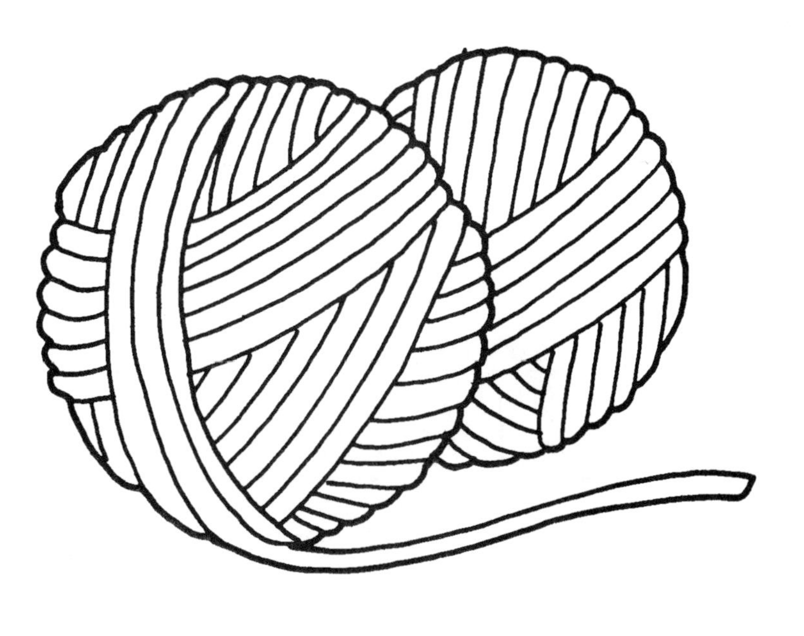

Y is for yarn

Yy

98

Y is for yak.

p56 © 1998 Totline® Publications

Yy

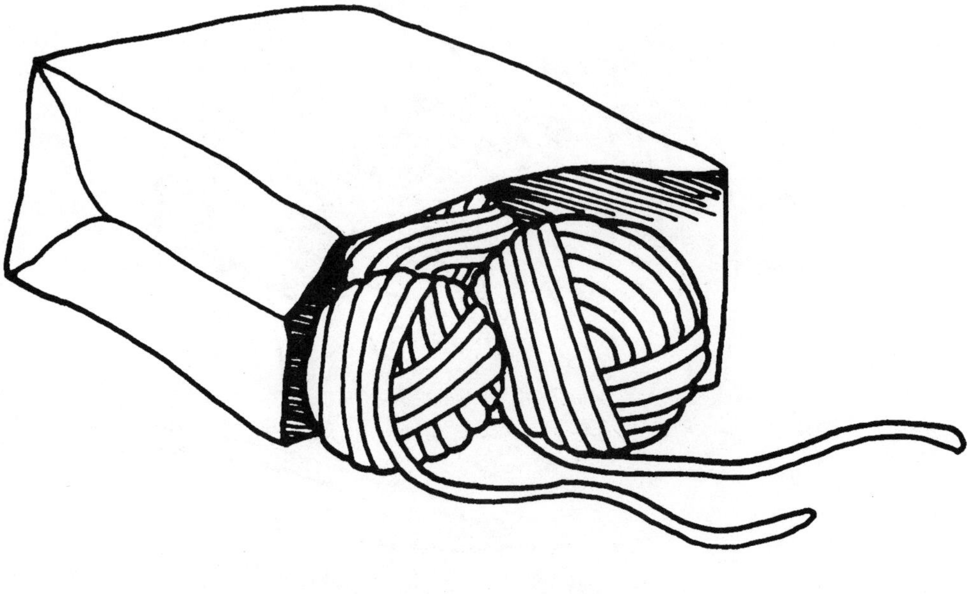

100

in my sack.

p56 © 1998 Totline® Publications

Zz

Z is for zebra.

Zz

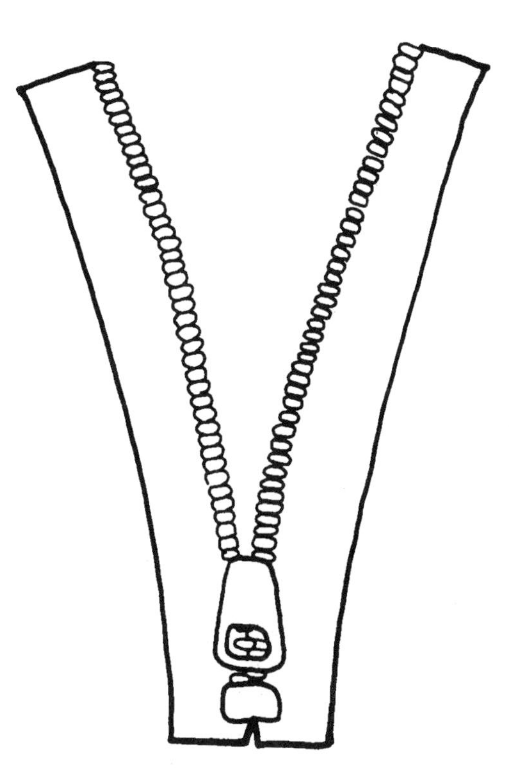

Z is for zipper

Zz

Z is for zoo.

Zz

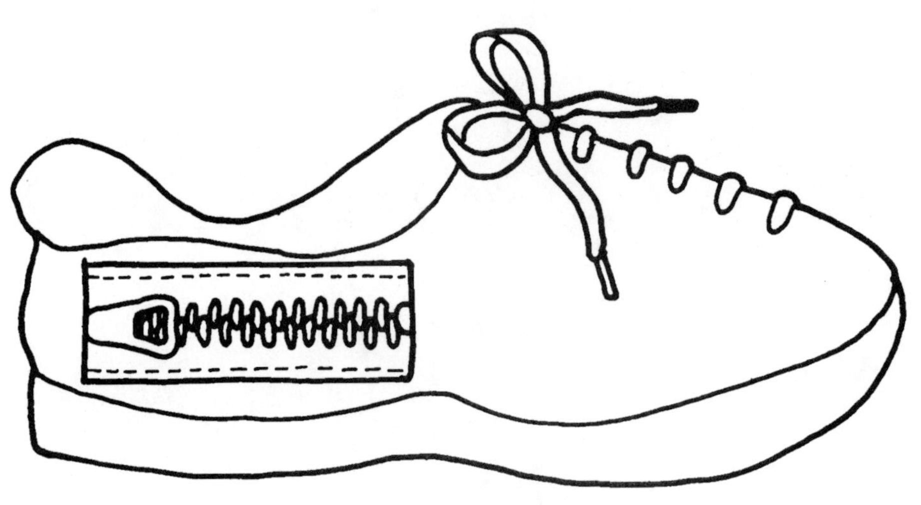

on my shoe.

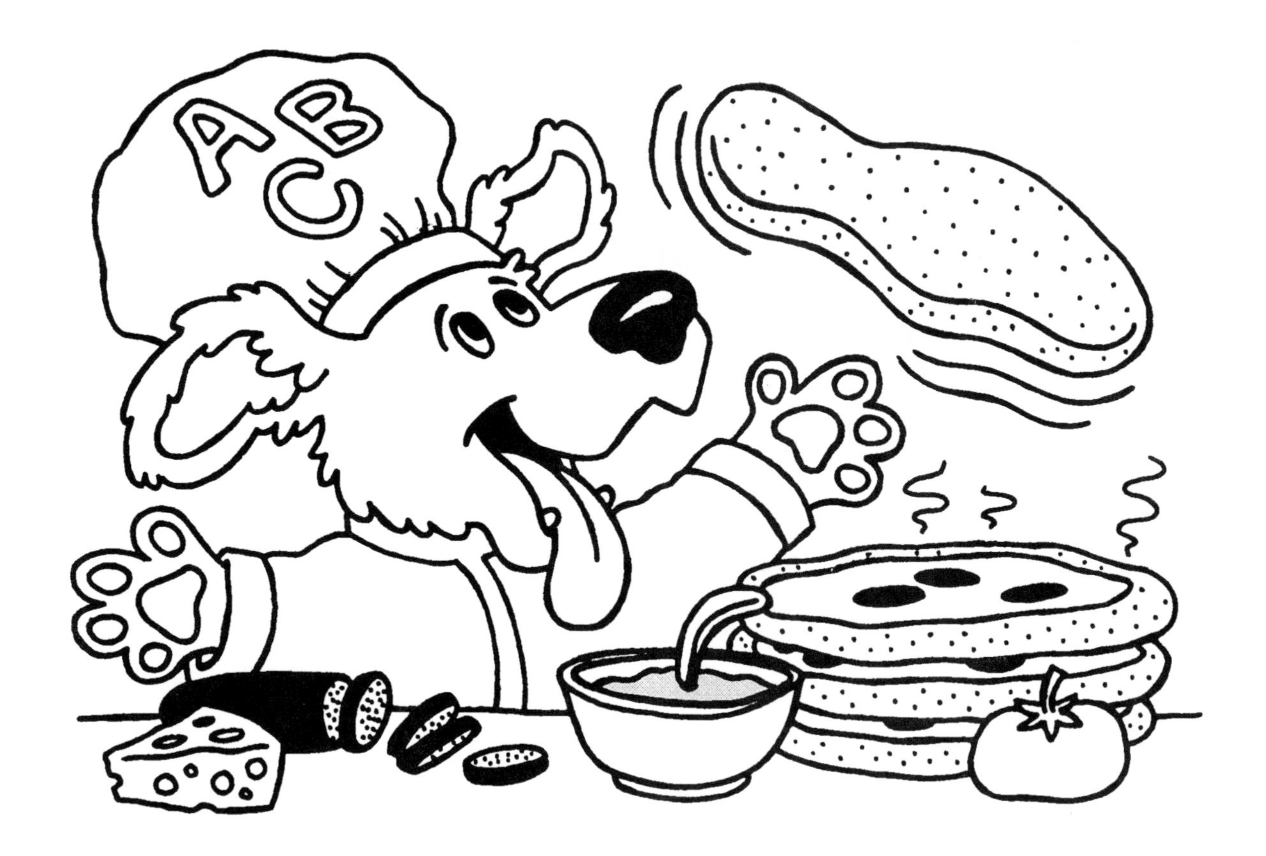

I made some pizzas.

Bb

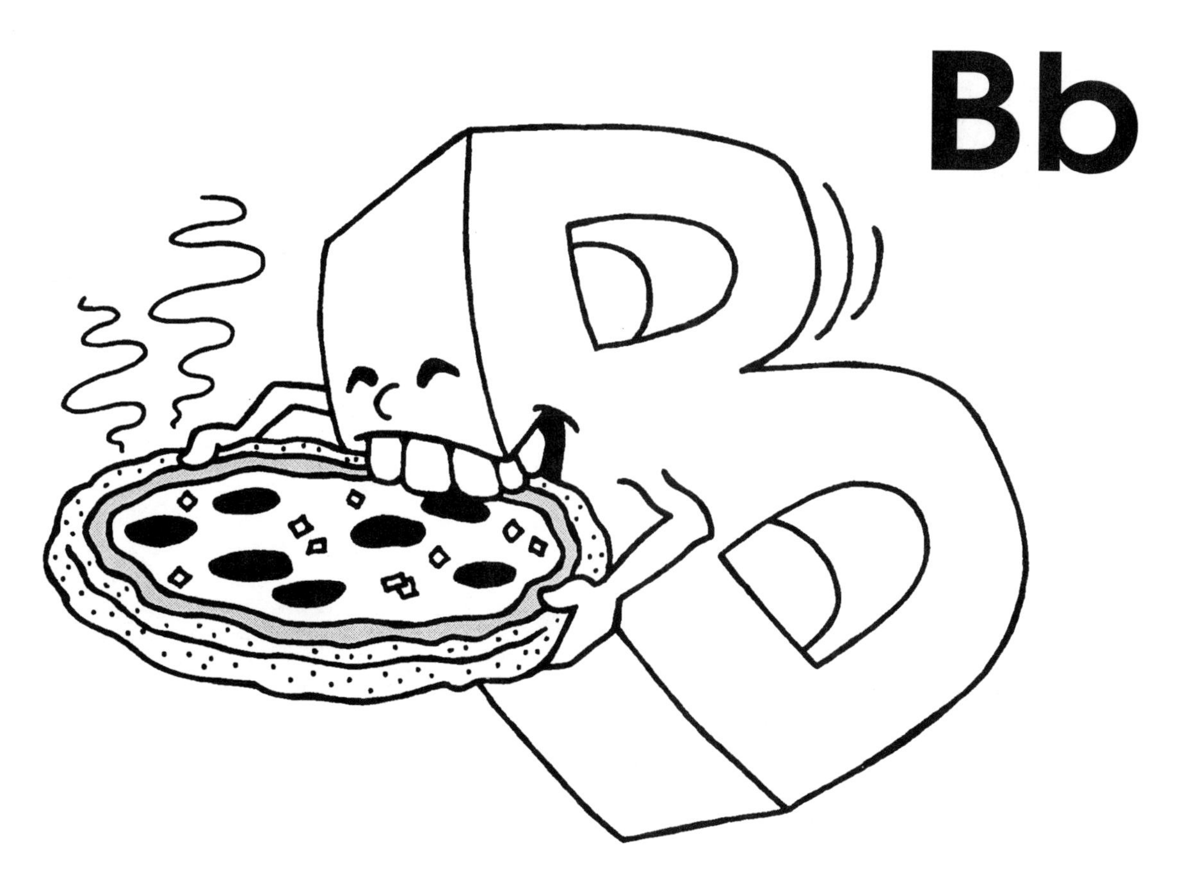

B bit a pizza.

Aa

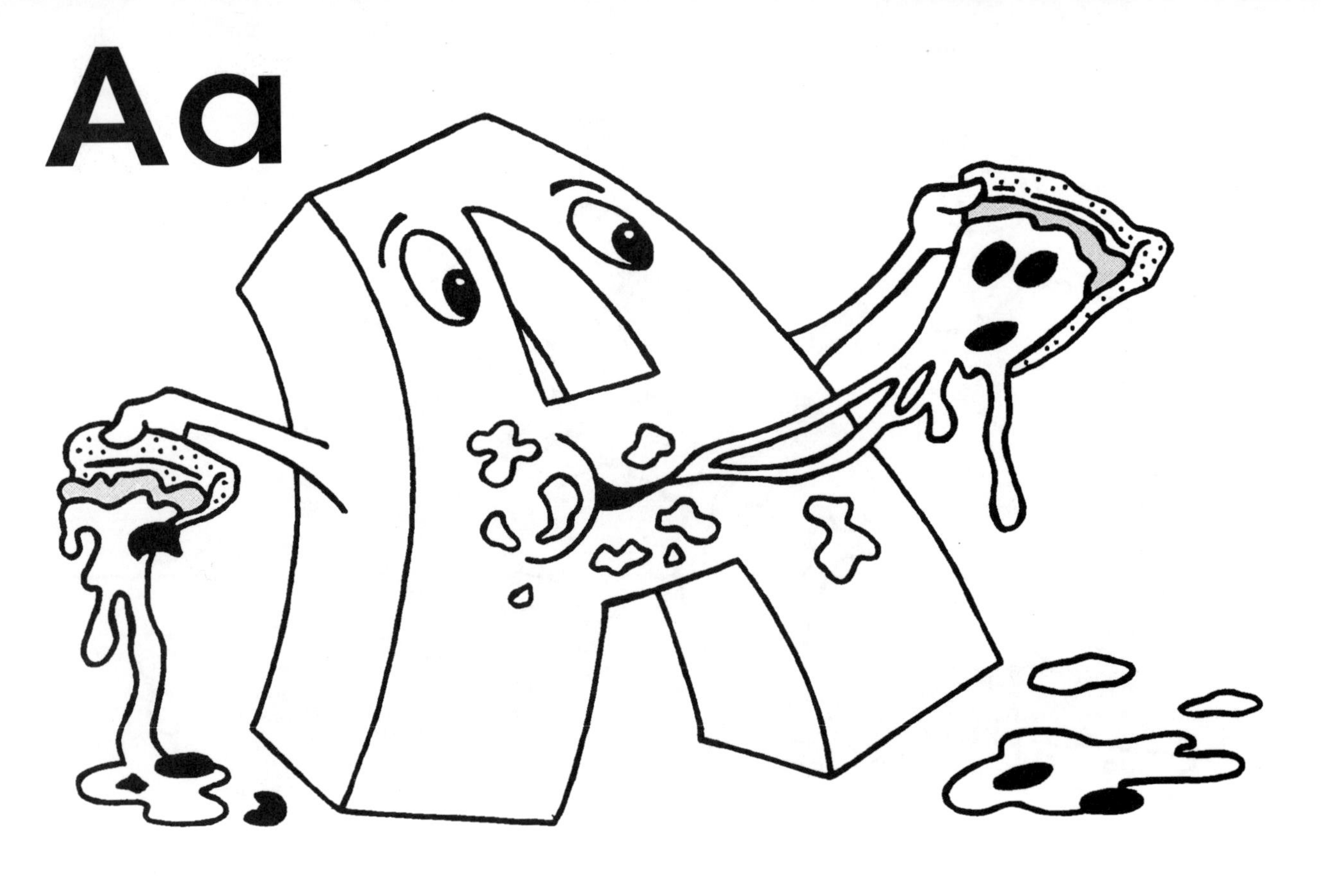

A ate a pizza.

p60 © 1998 Totline® Publications

Cc

C cut a pizza.

p60 © 1998 Totline® Publications

Dd

D dropped a pizza.

Ff

F found a pizza.

Ee

E enjoyed a pizza.

Gg

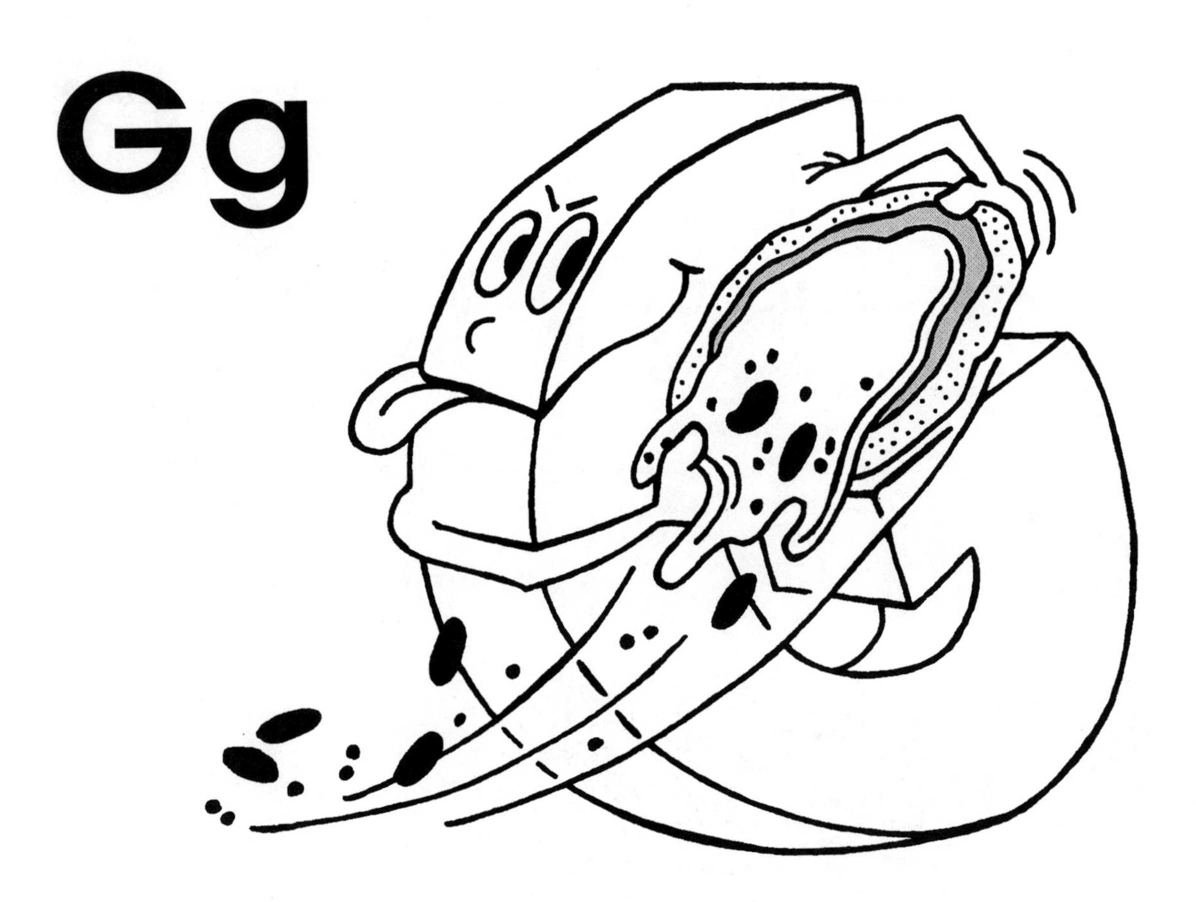

G grabbed a pizza.

Hh

H hid a pizza.

Jj

J jumped over a pizza.

Ii

I inspected a pizza.

Kk

K kicked a pizza.

Ll

L looked at a pizza.

Nn

N nibbled a pizza.

Mm

M made a pizza.

Oo

O ordered a pizza.

Pp

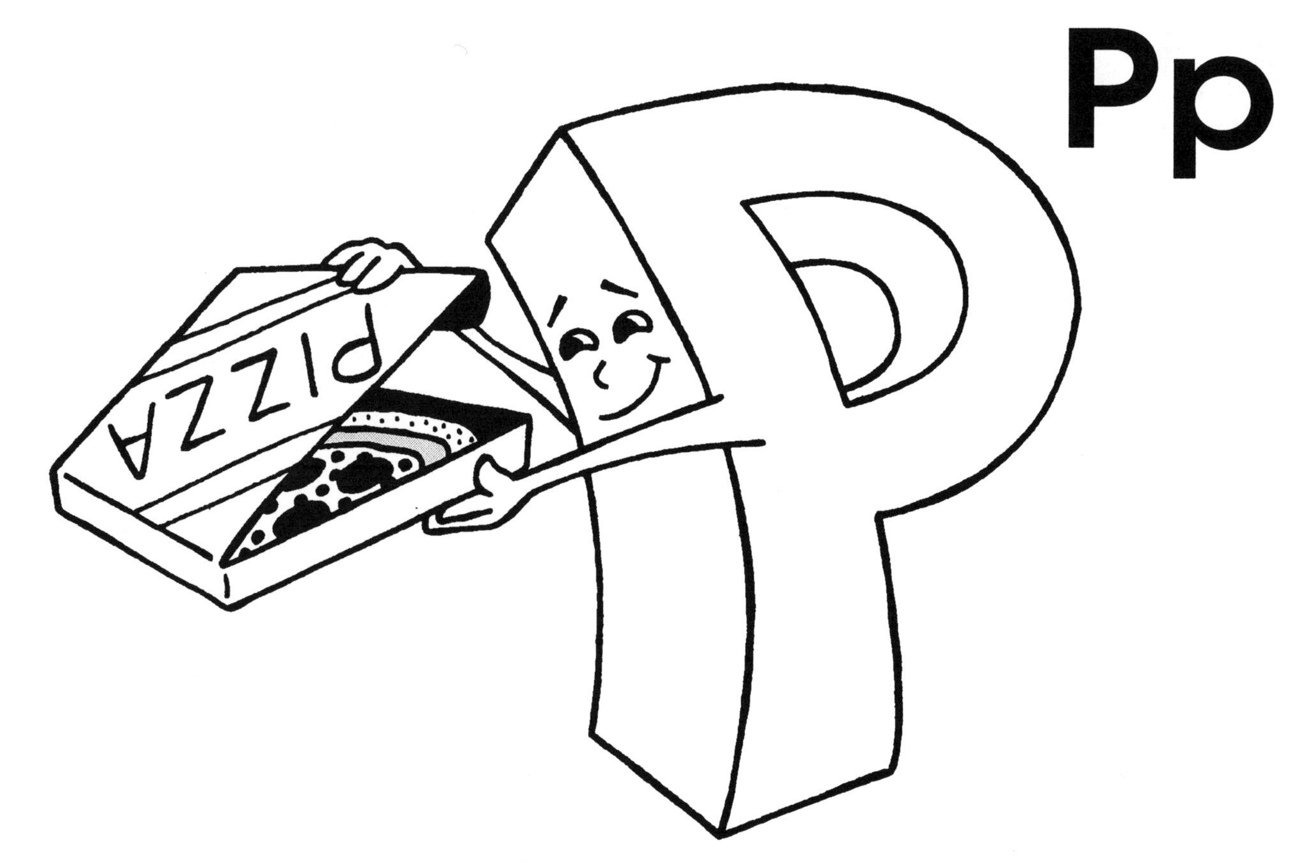

P peeked at a pizza.

p 67 © 1998 Totline® Publications

Rr

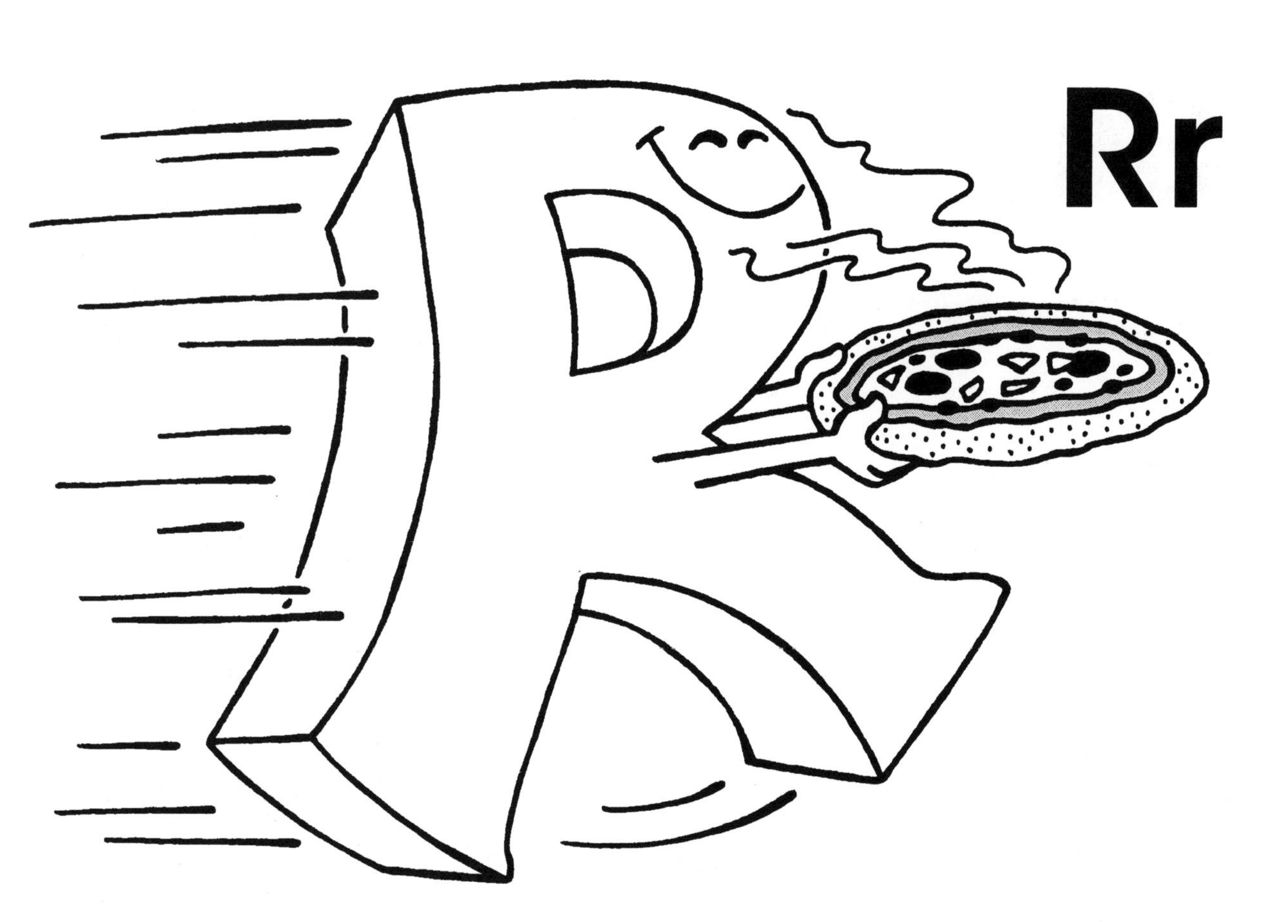

R ran off with a pizza.

Qq

18 ***Q*** **quartered a pizza.**

Ss

20 ***S*** **smelled a pizza.**

Tt

T tasted a pizza.

Uu Vv Ww Xx Yy Zz

U, V, and *W* invited *X, Y,* and *Z* to join them for a pizza party.

Aa

A **is for apple.**

Bb

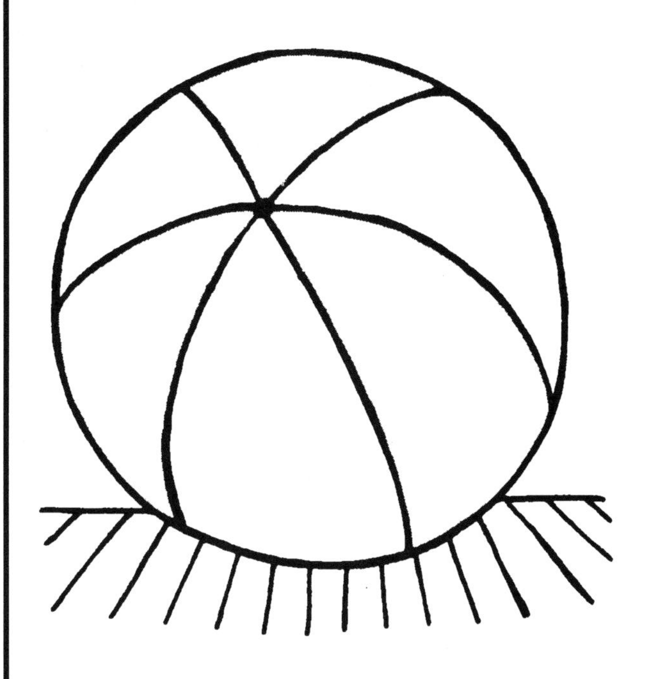

B **is for ball.**

p 71 © 1998 Totline® Publications

Ee

E **is for elephant.**

Ff

F **is for frog.**

Cc

 C is for candy.

Dd

D is for doll.

Gg

 G is for goose.

Hh

H is for hog.

p72 © 1998 Totline® Publications

Ii

I is for igloo.

Jj

J is for jam.

Mm

M is for monkey.

Nn

N is for nail.

Kk

K is for key.

Ll

L is for lamb.

Oo

O is for owl.

Pp

P is for pail.

p74 © 1998 Totline® Publications

Qq

Q **is for queen.**

Rr

R **is for rose.**

p 75 © 1998 Totline® Publications

Uu

U **is for umbrella.**

Vv

V **is for vase.**

Ss

10 *S* is for scissors.

Tt

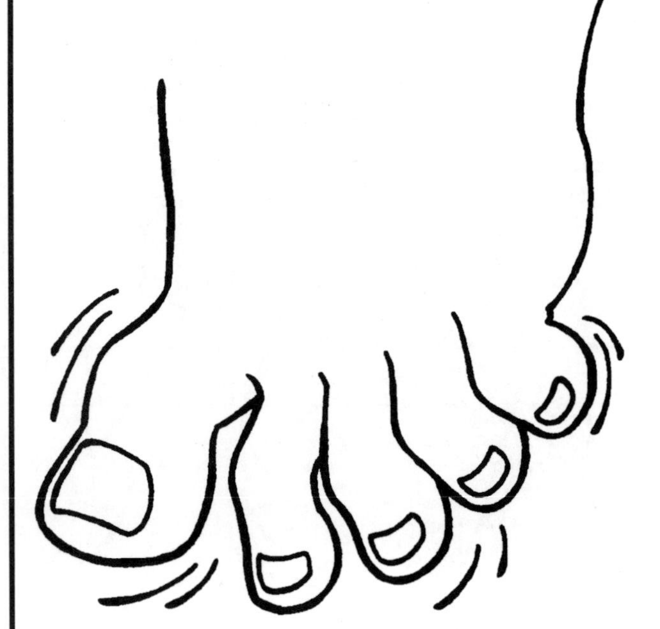

T is for toes.

Ww

W is for the wind
that blows on my face.

p76 © 1998 Totline® Publications

Xx

X is for x-ray.

Yy

Y is for you.

Zz

Z is for zebras in the zoo.

Totline® PUBLICATIONS

Teacher Resources

ART SERIES
Ideas for successful art experiences.
Cooperative Art
Special Day Art
Outdoor Art

BEST OF TOTLINE® SERIES
Totline's best ideas.
Best of Totline Newsletter
Best of Totline Bear Hugs
Best of Totline Parent Flyers

BUSY BEES SERIES
Seasonal ideas for twos and threes.
Fall • Winter • Spring • Summer

CELEBRATIONS SERIES
Early learning through celebrations.
Small World Celebrations
Special Day Celebrations
Great Big Holiday Celebrations
Celebrating Likes and Differences

CIRCLE TIME SERIES
Put the spotlight on circle time!
Introducing Concepts at Circle Time
Music and Dramatics at Circle Time
Storytime Ideas for Circle Time

EMPOWERING KIDS SERIES
Positive solutions to behavior issues.
Can-Do Kids
Problem-Solving Kids

EXPLORING SERIES
Versatile, hands-on learning.
Exploring Sand • Exploring Water

FOUR SEASONS
Active learning through the year.
Art • Math • Movement • Science

JUST RIGHT PATTERNS
8-page, reproducible pattern folders.
Valentine's Day • St. Patrick's Day • Easter • Halloween • Thanksgiving • Hanukkah • Christmas • Kwanzaa • Spring • Summer • Autumn • Winter • Air Transportation • Land Transportation • Service Vehicles • Water Transportation • Train • Desert Life • Farm Life • Forest Life • Ocean Life • Wetland Life • Zoo Life • Prehistoric Life

KINDERSTATION SERIES
Learning centers for kindergarten.
Calculation Station
Communication Station
Creation Station
Investigation Station

1•2•3 SERIES
Open-ended learning.
Art • Blocks • Games • Colors • Puppets • Reading & Writing • Math • Science • Shapes

1001 SERIES
Super reference books.
1001 Teaching Props
1001 Teaching Tips
1001 Rhymes & Fingerplays

PIGGYBACK® SONG BOOKS
New lyrics sung to favorite tunes!
Piggyback Songs
More Piggyback Songs
Piggyback Songs for Infants and Toddlers
Holiday Piggyback Songs
Animal Piggyback Songs
Piggyback Songs for School
Piggyback Songs to Sign
Spanish Piggyback Songs
More Piggyback Songs for School

PROJECT BOOK SERIES
Reproducible, cross-curricular project books and project ideas.
Start With Art
Start With Science

REPRODUCIBLE RHYMES
Make-and-take-home books for emergent readers.
Alphabet Rhymes • Object Rhymes

SNACKS SERIES
Nutrition combines with learning.
Super Snacks • Healthy Snacks • Teaching Snacks • Multicultural Snacks

TERRIFIC TIPS
Handy resources with valuable ideas.
Terrific Tips for Directors
Terrific Tips for Toddler Teachers
Terrific Tips for Preschool Teachers

THEME-A-SAURUS® SERIES
Classroom-tested, instant themes.
Theme-A-Saurus
Theme-A-Saurus II
Toddler Theme-A-Saurus
Alphabet Theme-A-Saurus
Nursery Rhyme Theme-A-Saurus
Storytime Theme-A-Saurus
Multisensory Theme-A-Saurus
Transportation Theme-A-Saurus
Field Trip Theme-A-Saurus

TODDLER RESOURCES
Great for working with 18 mos–3 yrs.
Playtime Props for Toddlers
Toddler Art

Parent Resources

A YEAR OF FUN SERIES
Age-specific books for parenting.
Just for Babies • Just for Ones • Just for Twos • Just for Threes • Just for Fours • Just for Fives

LEARN WITH PIGGYBACK® SONGS
Captivating music with age-appropriate themes.
Songs & Games for...
Babies • Toddlers • Threes • Fours
Sing a Song of...
Letters • Animals • Colors • Holidays • Me • Nature • Numbers

LEARN WITH STICKERS
Beginning workbook and first reader with 100-plus stickers.
Balloons • Birds • Bows • Bugs • Butterflies • Buttons • Eggs • Flags • Flowers • Hearts • Leaves • Mittens

MY FIRST COLORING BOOK
White illustrations on black backgrounds—perfect for toddlers!
All About Colors
All About Numbers
Under the Sea
Over and Under
Party Animals
Tops and Bottoms

PLAY AND LEARN
Activities for learning through play.
Blocks • Instruments • Kitchen Gadgets • Paper • Puppets • Puzzles

RAINY DAY FUN
This activity book for parent-child fun keeps minds active on rainy days!

RHYME & REASON STICKER WORKBOOKS
Sticker fun to boost language development and thinking skills.
Up in Space
All About Weather
At the Zoo
On the Farm
Things That Go
Under the Sea

SEEDS FOR SUCCESS
Ideas to help children develop essential life skills for future success.
Growing Creative Kids
Growing Happy Kids
Growing Responsible Kids
Growing Thinking Kids

THEME CALENDARS
Activities for every day.
Toddler Theme Calendar
Preschool Theme Calendar
Kindergarten Theme Calendar

TIME TO LEARN
Ideas for hands-on learning.
Colors • Letters • Measuring • Numbers • Science • Shapes • Matching and Sorting • New Words • Cutting and Pasting • Drawing and Writing • Listening • Taking Care of Myself

Posters

Celebrating Childhood Posters
Reminder Posters

Puppet Pals

Instant puppets!
Children's Favorites • The Three Bears • Nursery Rhymes • Old MacDonald • More Nursery Rhymes • Three Little Pigs • Three Billy Goats Gruff • Little Red Riding Hood

Manipulatives

CIRCLE PUZZLES
African Adventure Puzzle

LITTLE BUILDER STACKING CARDS
Castle • The Three Little Pigs

Tot-Mobiles

Each set includes four punch-out, easy-to-assemble mobiles.
Animals & Toys
Beginning Concepts
Four Seasons

Start right, start bright!

Totline products are available at parent and teacher stores.

NEW! Early Learning Resources

For Teachers

Art Series

Great ideas for exploring art with children ages 3 to 6! Easy, inexpensive activities encourage enjoyable art experiences in a variety of ways.

Cooperative Art • Outdoor Art • Special Day Art

The Best of Totline–Bear Hugs

This new resource is a collection of some of Totline's best ideas for fostering positive behavior.

Celebrating Childhood Posters

Inspire parents, staff, and yourself with these endearing posters with poems by Jean Warren.

The Children's Song
Patterns
Pretending
Snowflake Splendor
The Heart of a Child
Live Like the Child
The Light of Childhood
A Balloon
The Gift of Rhyme

Circle Time Series

Teachers will discover quick, easy ideas to incorporate into their lessons when they gather children together for this important time of the day.

Introducing Concepts at Circle Time
Music and Dramatics at Circle Time
Storytime Ideas for Circle Time

Empowering Kids

This unique series tackles behavioral issues in typical Totline fashion—practical ideas for empowering young children with self-esteem and basic social skills.

Problem-Solving Kids
Can-Do Kids

Theme-A-Saurus

Two new theme books join this popular Totline series!

Transportation Theme-A-Saurus
Field Trip Theme-A-Saurus

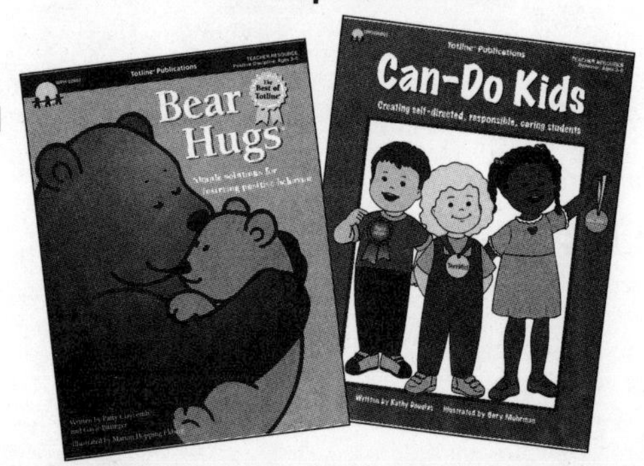

For Parents

My First Coloring Book Series

These coloring books are truly appropriate for toddlers—black backgrounds with white illustrations. That means no lines to cross and no-lose coloring fun! Bonus stickers included!

All About Colors
All About Numbers
Under the Sea
Over and Under
Party Animals
Tops and Bottoms

Happy Days

Seasonal fun with rhymes and songs, snack recipes, games, and arts and crafts.

Pumpkin Days • Turkey Days • Holly Days • Snowy Days

Little Builder Stacking Cards

Each game box includes 48 unique cards with different scenes printed on each side. Children can combine the cards that bend in the middle with the flat cards to form simple buildings or tall towers!

Castle
The Three Little Pigs

Rainy Day Fun

Turn rainy-day blahs into creative, learning fun! These creative Totline ideas turn a home into a jungle, post office, grocery store, and more!

Rhyme & Reason Sticker Workbooks

These age-appropriate workbooks combine language and thinking skills for a guaranteed fun learning experience. More than 100 stickers!

Up in Space • All About Weather • At the Zoo • On the Farm • Things That Go • Under the Sea

Theme Calendars

Weekly activity ideas in a nondated calendar for exploring the seasons with young children.

Toddler Theme Calendar
Preschool Theme Calendar
Kindergarten Theme Calendar

Totline products are available at fine parent and teacher stores.